Jennifer Plecas

# PRETEND

Philomel Books An Imprint of Penguin Group (USA) Inc.

For Tomislav,

the best, for real.

"Pretend," Jimmy said to Dad, "that this couch is a big boat, and that we're floating in the ocean."

"And pretend that there are sharks swimming all around us,
so we throw this magazine—I mean this rock—into the water,
and it scares them away. But now we're tired and starving,
and we don't know if we'll survive."

"Now you go," Jimmy said to Dad. "Say, 'Oh no,
what are we going to do?'"

Dad looked at Jimmy.

"Go ahead," Jimmy said.

"Oh no," Dad said. "What are we going to do?"

"I've got it!" said Jimmy. "I have these fishing lines.
They can save us!"

Jimmy and his dad cast their fishing lines into the water.

"Any bites?" Dad asked.

"I think so!" Jimmy cried. "It's not too big, but it will do!"

"I think I feel something too," Dad said.

"WHOA!" Jimmy said. "You got a big one!"

"I did!" said Dad, smiling.

"Now let's cook them," Jimmy said. "I'll start a little fire right here."

Jimmy and his dad cooked
their catch over the fire.
"Try yours," Jimmy said.
"See if it's ready."
"Not bad," Dad said.
Jimmy took a bite of his.

"Mmmmmmmmmmm!" he said. "It's just right."

Jimmy rubbed his belly and licked his lips.

"That was one good meal," he said. "Now let's search for land. We can't survive on this boat forever."

"No standing on the couch," said Dad.

"We're on a boat . . . ," Jimmy said.

Dad gave him a look.

Jimmy squatted. "Okay, how about we get our binoculars out?"

Dad searched his pockets.

"Right here," Jimmy said, "your binoculars."

"Oh," said Dad. "Here they are."

"See anything yet?" Jimmy asked.

"Is there something over there?" Dad asked.

Jimmy squinted into the distance.

"Yes!" Jimmy said. "I think I see it too! An island!
Paddle! Paddle fast!"

Jimmy and his dad paddled until they were
out of breath.

"I think we made it!" Dad said.

"I'll secure the boat for our landing," Jimmy said.

Dad hopped out after him.

"Ouch!" said Dad. "I think I stepped on a crab."

"OUCH!" cried Jimmy. "Me too! But don't stop! We've got to make it to shore! Help! Grab my hand!"

Jimmy flopped to the ground, panting.

"We made it!" Jimmy said. "Thanks for saving my life!"

"Anytime," Dad said.

Jimmy looked up. "You know, there are wild beasts that roam the bottom of this island," he said. "They eat people at night. The top is where we'll be safe. Let's climb to the top to make our fort."

Jimmy started to climb.

"I'll go first," he said.

"I don't know if I can
make it," Dad said.

"Don't worry!" Jimmy
called. "I'll help you!"

Jimmy and his dad rested
at the top of the mountain.

"We can see everything from up here,"
Jimmy said, looking through his binoculars again.
"Now we need to make our fort."

"We can use these huge leaves," Jimmy said. "We can put them on top of these tree stumps. It will protect us if it rains."

Together, Jimmy and his dad made a fort.

"It's good," Jimmy said. "Now we can go inside. Come on."

Jimmy and his dad crawled inside.

Inside, the fort was nice and cool.

"I think it might be time for a rest," Dad said, stretching out as best he could. "I have an idea. Why don't we pretend that we're two tired explorers taking a rest in their fort after a long day of exploring?"

"Let's pretend that the stars are coming out, and we're building a campfire," Jimmy said. "And then we can look up at the stars and say, 'This is the best time ever.'"

"Well," said Dad, "I don't have to pretend that part.

It *is* the best time ever."

Jimmy got to work quickly. He started the fire.

It was nice and warm.

"You're a pretty good pretender, Dad," Jimmy said.

"So are you," said Dad. "And you're pretty good for real."

Jimmy smiled. "You too, Dad," he said. "You're the best.

For pretend and for real."

# PHILOMEL BOOKS

A division of Penguin Young Readers Group. Published by The Penguin Group.
Penguin Group (USA) Inc., 375 Hudson Street, New York, NY 10014, U.S.A.
Penguin Group (Canada), 90 Eglinton Avenue East, Suite 700, Toronto, Ontario M4P 2Y3, Canada (a division of Pearson Penguin Canada Inc.).
Penguin Books Ltd, 80 Strand, London WC2R ORL, England.
Penguin Ireland, 25 St. Stephen's Green, Dublin 2, Ireland (a division of Penguin Books Ltd).
Penguin Group (Australia), 250 Camberwell Road, Camberwell, Victoria 3124, Australia (a division of Pearson Australia Group Pty Ltd).
Penguin Books India Pvt Ltd, 11 Community Centre, Panchsheel Park, New Delhi – 110 017, India.
Penguin Group (NZ), 67 Apollo Drive, Rosedale, North Shore 0632, New Zealand (a division of Pearson New Zealand Ltd).
Penguin Books (South Africa) (Pty) Ltd, 24 Sturdee Avenue, Rosebank, Johannesburg 2196, South Africa.
Penguin Books Ltd, Registered Offices: 80 Strand, London WC2R ORL, England.

Design by Semadar Megged.   Text set in Providence Sans.   The illustrations are rendered in ink and watercolor.
Library of Congress Cataloging-in-Publication Data
Plecas, Jennifer.   Pretend / Jennifer Plecas.   p. cm.   Summary: A father and son embark on an imaginary adventure and discover how much they love each other.
[1. Imagination—Fiction. 2. Fathers and sons—Fiction.] I. Title.   PZ7.P7173Pr 2011   [E]—dc22   2010019288
ISBN 978-0-399-23430-9
1 3 5 7 9 10 8 6 4 2